Who Was Born This Special Day?

Eve Bunting

✿ *and* ✿

Leonid Gore

ATHENEUM BOOKS *for* YOUNG READERS

NEW YORK   LONDON   TORONTO   SYDNEY   SINGAPORE

Atheneum Books for Young Readers
An imprint of Simon & Schuster Children's Publishing Division
1230 Avenue of the Americas
New York, New York 10020

Book design by Angela Carlino

The text of this book is set in Vendetta Medium.

The illustrations are rendered in acrylic paint on paper.

Printed in Hong Kong

2 4 6 8 10 9 7 5 3 1

32530 605318938

Library of Congress Cataloging-in-Publishing Data

Bunting, Eve, 1928-
Who was born this special day?/ by Eve Bunting; illustrations by Leonid Gore.
p. cm.
Summary: Not the lamb or the goat or the donkey or the dove was born on the first Christ-
mas long ago, but a special child was.
ISBN 0-689-82302-9
1. Jesus Christ Juvenile poetry. 2. Children's poetry, American. 3. Christian poetry, American.
[1. Jesus Christ—Nativity Poetry. 2. American poetry.] I. Gore, Leonid, ill. II. Title.
PS3552.U4735W48 2000 811'.54—dc21 99-27675

FIRST
EDITION

E BUNT

To my daughter Christine
—E. B.

For Harriet, with appreciation
—L. G.

*W*ho was born this special day?

Was it you, little lamb?

"I was born back in early May
when the breezes of spring chased winter away."

It was not the lamb.

Was it you, little goat?

"No, not I.
I was born on a soft, warm night
under the white of the moon's pale light."

It was not the goat.

Who was born this special day?
Was it you, little calf?

"I breathed first in a barn where I lay,
safe in the warmth of the sweet-smelling hay."

It was not the calf.

Someone was born this special day.
Was it you, little donkey?

The donkey snug in his coat of gray
shakes his head in a donkey way.

It was not the donkey.

Were you born this day, mourning dove?

"No, not I.
I was born in a nest of love
with leaves that whispered and sang above."

It was not the dove.

Is it your birthday, cedar tree?
"No, not mine.

When I was a seedling floating in space,
a wandering wind dropped me here in this place."

It was not the tree.

Was it you, little stone?
"No, not I.

I've been here since the world began
part of the great Creation plan."

It was not the stone.

Who was born this special day?

Was it the child?
The child who lies in the manger bed,
the shine of the star high overhead?

Clouds filled with angels shimmering bright,
singing of joy this dear, holy night.
Who was born this special day?

It was the child.